H.L. Hosmer

Early History of the Maumee Valley

SALZWASSER
VERLAG

H.L. Hosmer

Early History of the Maumee Valley

Reprint of the original, first published in 1858.

1st Edition 2023 | ISBN: 978-3-37514-874-4

Verlag (Publisher): Salzwasser Verlag GmbH, Zeilweg 44, 60439 Frankfurt, Deutschland
Vertretungsberechtigt (Authorized to represent): E. Roepke, Zeilweg 44, 60439 Frankfurt, Deutschland
Druck (Print): Books on Demand GmbH, In de Tarpen 42, 22848 Norderstedt, Deutschland

EARLY HISTORY

OF THE

Maumee Valley.

BY H. L. HOSMER.

———•◆•———

TOLEDO:
PUBLISHED BY HOSMER & HARRIS,
1858.

HISTORY.

Previous to the decisive battle of Gen. Wayne in 1794, the Maumee Valley was the favorite home of the Indian. Here, for ages he had lived unmolested—roaming through forests and beside streams that invited and rewarded his pursuits—in possession of a soil which yielded abundantly to his careless tillage and cultivation. Here, were the graves of his ancestors for many generations, and the spots consecrated in his affections by recollections and events, which rendered them as dear to him as life itself. Here, he had often lighted the council fire, and listened to the indignant denunciations of his brethren against the pale faces. Here, forces had been organized for predatory and offensive warfare, and the fearful war whoop and hideous scalp dance had often proclaimed how successful had been their bloody enterprise. This beautiful valley was to the Indian enchanted ground. He never left it for the briefest period without regret, or returned to it without delight. The gurgling of the river as it broke into rapids over the rifted rocks—the soughing of the wind through the mighty forests—the drumming of the partridge at mid-day, and the prolonged midnight howl of the wolf were sweeter music to his ears, than any he ever listened to elsewhere. Here, the Indian maidens were more beautiful, and the gallants of the sterner sex more manly and daring. Mighty nations, not unlike in number and prowess the mighty nations of old, rose, flourished and fell here, amid the scenes which had witnessed their combats, and the remnants which had struggled for their supremacy. The world contained no other spot around which the Ottawas and Miamis had gathered so many endearments—no other, indeed, which even, for purposes of enterprise or ambition, they were willing to exchange for it. Not only were they contented—they were delighted to dwell amid the varied scenery of River, Rock and Island, and like the Arcadian shepherds, they refused, until refusal was unavailing, to abandon it to their enemies. Mournful and melancholy is the story of their decay—full of sadness and gloom the reflections it suggests to the mind which sorrows for their fate—sorrows, while it cannot aid, nor find aug'ht in the exchange to regret.

For a long period before the battle of 1794, traders from Canada, and refugees, had taken up an abode with the Indians of this valley—and at their instigation much of the border massacre occurred, which led to the various ill-fated expeditions of Dunmore, Crawford, Harmer and St. Clair, and to the final and terribly retributive onslaught of Gen. Wayne. Simon Girty, the noted renegade, abandoned the house he had long occupied, above Napoleon, and fled to Canada before the invading army. An Indian agent, no less celebrated, one Colonel McKee, to whom, at that time and afterwards, in 1812, we were indebted for many of the bloodiest depredations of the savages, dwelt near the present site of Maumee city, where his barns, stores, and other property were destroyed by our indignant soldiery. A strong fortress—Fort Miami—had been erected by the Canadian Governor, Simcoe, a short time before the battle, fifty miles within the recognized boundary between the possessions of Great Britain and the United States, and was at the time under the command of a testy Scotch Major, by the name of Campbell.

The March of Gen. Wayne into the Indian country had been so stealthy, that it won for him the name of the Black Snake. He had not only advanced by an obscure and difficult route, but had attempted to divert the attention of the Indians by clearing out two roads in the direction of their country and taking neither. His generalship, however, did not escape the vigilance of the famous Miami Chief, Little Turtle, who, when Wayne entered the valley of the Maumee, was prepared with Miamis, Wyandots, Pottawatamies, Delawares, Shawnese, Chippewas, Ottawas and Senecas, to the number of two thousand, to give him battle. The Continental Legion under Gen. Wayne was of about equal strength, exclusive of eleven hundred mounted Kentuckians under Gen. Scott. As soon as he came so near the savages as to render a battle unavoidable, except by friendly negotiation, Wayne sent to them an envoy of peace, whom they received with every demonstration of hostility, and would have slain, but that some of their warriors were prisoners in the American camp. The battle was not delayed—and it resulted in the loss of one hundred and seven Americans, and in the total rout of the Indians. Their loss, never accurately known, was supposed to exceed a thousand.

A council was held by the several Chiefs the night preceding the engagement, at which, Little Turtle recommended the acceptance of the terms of peace offered by Gen. Wayne. "We have beaten the enemy," said he, "twice under separate commanders. We cannot expect the same good fortune always to attend us. The Americans are now led by a chief who never sleeps. The night and the day are alike to him, and during all the time that he has been marching upon our villages, notwithstanding the watchfulness of our young men, we have never been able to surprise him. Think well of it. There is something whispers me it would be prudent to listen to the offers of peace." He was reproached with cowardice. Stung to the quick, he said no more, but took part in the battle, performing his duty with wonted bravery.

Major Campbell addressed a note to Gen. Wayne the day after the battle, expressing surprise at the appearance of an American force within gun-shot of his batteries, and desiring to be informed in what light he should regard such audacity.

Wayne, in his reply, says "that the most full and satisfactory answer was announced the day before from the muzzle of his small arms, in an action with a horde of savages in the vicinity of the Fort, and which terminated gloriously to the American arms. But," he adds, "had it continued until .the Indians were driven under the influence of the Fort and guns mentioned, they would not much have impeded the progress of the victorious army under my command, as no such post was established at the commencement of the present war between the Indians and the United States." Campbell rejoined, complaining that armed Americans should come within pistol-shot of his works, and threatened hostilities should such insults to his Majesty's flag be continued. Wayne reconnoitered the Fort closely in every direction, and found it to be a strong, regular work, with two bastions mounting eight pieces of artillery on the rear face, and four upon the front, facing the river. He then wrote to the British commander, disclaiming any desire to resort to hostile measures, but denouncing the erection of the Fort, as an act of decided aggression towards the United States, and requiring his instant departure from our territory. Campbell answered that he should only leave when commanded to by those under whom he served, and again warned the American General not to approach within reach of his guns. The only notice Wayne took of this last letter, was to cause everything of a combustible nature, for miles around the Fort, to be set on fire, and all the corn fields and vegetable patches to be destroyed. This failed to provoke the wary Scot into any more decided acts of hostility, than the utterance of a few threats and oaths. Restricted by his instructions from attacking any British posts he might find within the American lines, unless they first assumed a belligerent attitude, Wayne chafed for a pretext to pay his respects to the Briton. It is reported that on one occasion, he ordered one of his grenadiers to descend the bank in front of the Fort, and bring a pail of water from the river.

"Why, General," replied the soldier, "were I to do so, they would shoot me from the Fort."

"That's the very thing I want them to do, John," replied Mad Anthony, "let them kill you, and we'll massacre every soul of 'em."

The American army returned to the camp Grand Glaize, where Wayne, on his downward march, had constructed Fort Defiance, after a stay of three days at the foot of the rapids. The whole Indian country along the Maumee and Auglaize rivers, which Wayne wrote "appeared like one continued village for many miles," was laid waste, and forts erected to protect it against the Indians. On being informed of the defeat of the Indians, Governor Simcoe hastened from Niagara to Fort Miami, accompanied by Capt. Brant, the great chief of the Six Nations, and held a council with the Indians on the 30th September, 1794. They had already intimated a desire to Wayne, to negotiate a peace, but the arch counsels of Simcoe and Brant caused them to hesitate, and for a while the prospect was fair for another campaign of active hostilities. In the meantime, however, the difficulties between the United States and Great Britain were adjusted by Jay's Treaty, so that the Indians were forsaken by their British allies. Wayne's victory had quieted the restlessness of the Six Nations, who refused any further calls for assistance to their western brethren, and at this critical juncture the Treaty of Greenville was concluded, and the long and destructive war, which, for so many years had desolated the frontier, was brought to a satisfactory termination. Capt. Brant, in a speech made not long afterwards, said: "The Indians, convinced by those in the Miami Fort, and other circumstances, that they were mistaken in their expectations of any assistance from Great Britain, did not longer oppose the Americans with their wonted unanimity. The consequence was that Gen. Wayne, by the peaceable language he held to them, induced them to hold a treaty at his own head-quarters, in which he concluded a peace entirely on his own terms."

A small stockade, known by the name of Fort Industry, was built near' the junction of Swan Creek and the Maumee, immediately after the treaty of Greenville. It was garrisoned until 1808 by about 150 men, merely to guard the territory ceded to the United States, against Indian depredations.

Such was the valley of the lower Maumee until after the battle of 1794. What it was for some years after that event may be gathered from the following extracts, from one of Judge Burnet's letters to the Ohio Historical Society:

"My yearly trips to Detroit from 1796 to 1802 made it necessary to pass through some of the Indian towns, and convenient to visit many of them. Of course I had frequent opportunities of seeing thousands of them in their villages and at their hunting camps, and of forming an acquaintance with some of their distinguished Chiefs. I have eat and slept in their towns and partaken of their hospitality, which had no limit but that of their contracted means.

" In journeying more recently through the State, in discharging my judicial duties, I sometimes passed over the ground on which I had seen towns filled with happy families of that devoted race, without perceiving the smallest trace of what had once been there. All their ancient settlements on the route to Fort Defiance, and from thence to the foot of the rapids, had been broken up and deserted. The battle ground of Gen. Wayne, which I had often seen in the rude state in which it was when the decisive action of 1794 was fought, was so altered and changed that I could not recognize it, and not an indication remained of the very extensive Indian settlements which I had formerly seen there. It seemed almost impossible that in so short a period, such an astonishing change could have taken place."

Peter Navarre, a grandson of Robert de Navarre, a French officer, who came to America in 1745, and was appointed Notaire Royal and Sub-Deligue, on the early establishment of Detroit, was born in Detroit, and came with his father's family to reside at the mouth of the Maumee in 1807. At that time the Indians of the Ottawa nation lived in a neat little village, nearly opposite Manhattan. Navarre says it was a grassy plat—the houses, of logs, about sixty in number, were built in two rows, white-washed, and presented a cheerful and pleasant appearance. The village had been in existence since the days of Pontiac, and marked the site of his encampment on the Maumee, at the time he left Detroit in 1764. The head Chief of the nation, Tish-qua-gwun, was a descendant from Pontiac. The character generally given to him, by those who knew him, was that of a kind-hearted, peaceable old man. Assouga was the name of another village Chief of considerable character. At this time, also, the widow of Pontiac, Kan-tuck-ee-gun, and his son, Otussa, dwelt at the mouth of the river. The old woman was held in great reverence, always the first one applied to by the nations for advice, and the first to sign all treaties. Otussa was a man of excellent sense, free from the vices of his tribe, and with none of the ferocity, inherited all the bravery of his father. He was a proud man, and held intercourse with those of the whites only, who, like himself, were distinguished for station or power. Mesh-ke-ma, a cousin of Otussa, was a Chief on the opposite side of the river. He was the finest orator in the nation, and the foremost speaker at all treaties. Ka-ne-wa-ba was another noted Chief. A-be-e-wa, also a Chief, was a good speaker and a man of fine sense. He was quite young at the time of his death, which was occasioned by poison, as early as 1810. Navarre's recollections of him seem to indicate that he was the most talented man in the nation. There were eight thousand of the Ottawas at this time living upon the lower Maumee. They lived principally by hunting and fishing. Once a year they had a sacrifice of the best of everything they owned. On such occasions, which generally lasted three days, they would eat what they could, and burn the remnant of their food, so that the dogs could not get it. About ten days before this annual sacrifice, they would blacken their faces, and eat and drink only in the afternoon. Thousands of them would finally assemble, and erect a shanty, where they held their feast. They would make religious speeches with the upraised hand on these occasions, and by every outward demonstration testify their reverence for the Great Spirit.

Feasts were frequent among them, and upon various occasions. Sometimes sickness, often hunting—and oftener still, to enjoy the pleasures of a protracted season of ball-playing, they would have feasts of several days continuance. They drank but little liquor, at this period, were proud and vain, and many of them rich. Their robes were of fine cloths bedizened with silver and gold coin, which jingled and glittered as they walked. Often the chiefs would have several hundred dollars fastened to their dresses.

A variety of dances were incident to the feasts. One called Ki-a-wa, indicated the approach of war, and was only employed as an amusement one or two years before war was expected. This dance was very constantly introduced on festive occasions, for two years before the war of 1812.

Ne-gan-e-ga was a dance for pleasure, and was accompanied by much that was sportive and gleesome in gesture and motion.

The grand calumet dance, was in time of peace danced with a large white pipe, but when war raged or was expected, the pipe was red, or substituted entirely by the tomahawk. A white pipe was never used in this dance, after 1810 until the war was closed.

Met-a-wee, a medicine dance, was introduced on occasions of sickness, for the purpose of propitiating the anger of the Great Spirit.

The English visited the Indians in great numbers during the years 1810 and 1811, for the purpose of interesting them in a contemplated war against America. Navarre saw them frequently—heard their counsels and witnessed their effects upon the nation. From that time they began to deteriorate—liquor was introduced among them in large quantities, and other vices were soon developed.

The Indian titles to the lands in the valley, by the negotiations made at the numerous treaties which, from 1796 to 1810, followed each other in close succession, was finally frittered away, until a few acres were all that the tribes possessed. Treaties and whiskey had achieved greater victories for the nation than the guns of Wayne. The poor Indians became aliens in the land of their fathers. Of them—or rather of the miserable remnant of them, which dissipation and the sword had spared, for many years before they finally left the valley—it might have been written:

"Where'er their vagrant footsteps roam,
They're strangers in a desert home."

In no part of the United States has the *paternal* policy pursued by our Government towards the Indians been productive of greater evil and hardship to them than in this valley. They have here, through the agency of the usual incidents to treaties and payments been literally robbed of everything. The last hundred of the once powerful tribe of Ottawas, who left their old homes in 1837, to go West of the Mississippi, were nothing but vagrants and drunkards—made so by contact with the whites, who did not scruple to flatter, wheedle and deceive, so long as there was aught to gain by it, nor to expel with indecent haste, when they had despoiled them of all their possessions.

The peace of this valley, after the treaty of Greenville, was not disturbed until 1808. During that year, Ellsk-wa-ta-wa, the famous Shawanese Prophet, and brother of Tecumseh, took possession of a tract near the junction of the Tippecanoe and Wabash rivers, where, by claiming to have received a commission from the Great Spirit, he induced a large number of Wyandots, Shawanese, Ottawas and Pottawatamies to assemble for the avowed purpose of retaking the land they had ceded to the United States. This band of hostile Indians, through the

2

almost superhuman exertions of Tecumseh to unite the western
and Southern tribes, gradually increased in numbers until
they thought themselves sufficiently formidable to cope with
any army the whites could send against them. Their first
demonstrations were made against the Miamis, who would not
unite with them. Some two hundred of the Ottawas of the
lower Maumee, including several noted Chiefs, left their villages
and took up their residence with the Prophet. Gen. Harrison,
then Governor, at Vincennes, and Gen. Hull, Governor at
Detroit, strove by pacific measures to prevent the shedding of
blood, but the entire Indian country was at this time filled with
Canadian Traders, who, being in the British interest, spared
no opportunity to revive the ancient prejudices of the Savages
against the Americans, and infuse new ones into their minds.
White settlements, which before this time had commenced in
this valley, were deserted, and for a while, an immediate out-
break was anticipated.

The following speech of Gen. Harrison to the Miamis and
the replies by Richardville and other Chiefs of that nation,
which were delivered sometime after the prophet commenced
operations, show how little confidence existed between the
Whites and the Indians, and what was at this time the intention
of Gov. Harrison respecting them :

My Children. You had left this place but two days, when
I received letters from your Great Father, the President of
the seventeen fires, and it was my wish that you should know
what they contained, because their contents were of consequence to you. I sent after you one of your own people,
inviting you to return. You not only refused to do so, but
you insulted my messenger. You insulted me, and the Great
Chief of the Seventeen Fires, whom I represent. You told
him the letters which I had pretended to have received were
forgeries.

My Children. This conduct of yours has grieved me much,
and my anger against you was for a while very great, but I

have now cast it off, and I feel nothing but pity for you, and anger against those who have deceived you. I now speak to you in the name of your Father of the Seventeen Fires. Listen to me.

My Children. My eyes are now open and I am now looking towards the Wabash. I see a dark cloud hanging over it. Those who raised it intended it for my destruction, but I will turn it on their own heads.

My Children. I hoped that you would not be injured by this cloud. You have seen it gathering. You had timely notice to keep clear of it. The thunder begins to roll, take care that it does not burst upon your heads.

My Children. I now speak plain to you. What is that great collection of people at the mouth of the Tippecanoe intended for? I am not blind, my children. I can easily see what their object is. These people have boasted that they will find me asleep, but they will be deceived.

My Children. Do not suppose that I am foolish enough to suffer them to go on with their preparations until they are ready to strike my people. No. I have watched their motions. I know what they wish to do, and you know it also. Listen, then, to what I say. I will not suffer any more strange Indians to settle on the Wabash. Those that are there, and do not belong there shall disperse and go to their own tribes.

My Children. When you made the treaty with Gen. Wayne, you promised that if you knew of any parties of Indians passing through your country with hostile intentions towards us, that you would give us notice of it and endeavor to stop them. I now inform you that I consider all those who join the Prophet and his party as hostile, and I call upon you to fulfill your engagements. I have also sent to the tribes which have any of their warriors with the Prophet to withdraw them immediately. Those who do not comply, I shall consider to have let go the chain of friendship which united us.

My Children. Be wise, and listen to my voice. I fear that

you have got on a road that will lead you to destruction. It is not yet too late to turn back. Have pity upon your women and children. It is time that my friends should be known. I must draw a line. Those that keep me by the hand must be on one side of it, and those that adhere to the Prophet, the other.

My Children. Take your choice. My warriors are in motion, but they shall do you no hurt unless you force me to it; but I must have satisfaction for the murder of my people, and the war pole that has been raised on the Wabash must be taken down.

My Children. Let me know your determination by Mr. Dubois. He will explain to you everything. Do not suffer bad advice to mislead you. Throw yourselves into the arms of your father and he will receive you and nourish you. Do not be afraid to speak your minds. Tell those people that have settled on the Wabash without your leave, that the land is yours and you do not wish them there. Do not be afraid to say this. You shall be supported. My warriors are getting ready, and, if it is necessary, you shall see an army of them at your backs, more numerous than the leaves of the trees."

Lapussia, or Richardville, one of the head chiefs of the Miami Nation, made the following reply, which is not more adroit than most of the business transactions of this noted man:

"Governor Harrison: You that reside at Vincennes, listen to what I say. You wish to hear what I have to say. At Vincennes we heard you speak, when we stood as we now stand. You now tell us we are on a wrong road—a road that will lead us to destruction. You are deceived. We are not on a wrong road. While I was walking along, I heard you speak concerning the Prophet. You say that we are of his party. I hold you both by the hand. I don't hold the Shawnee tight. You have both told one story. You say if we would listen to you, we would be happy. The hearts of the Miamis are good. The Great Spirit has put us on a good and fertile land. We are now anxiously waiting to hear who tells us the truth for the first time.

Father. Your eyes are open. When you cast your eyes on your children you see that they are poor. They have not the necessaries of life. We want ammunition to support our women and children. That has compelled us to take this journey.

Father. We have not let you go. We yet hold you. We yet hold you by the hand—neither do we hold the hand of the Prophet with a view of injuring you. I therefore tell you, that you are not correct when you tell us we have joined hands with the Prophet to injure you.

Father. I listened to you a few days ago, when you told me of the depredations committed on the Mississippi. I told you that neither I or my people had any wish to assist that party —that we loved your people, that it gave us pleasure to see them standing around—a pleasure of which we should be deprived by making war upon them, as war would be destructive to both parties.

Father. You have always told me that you were, by our Great Father, placed here among the red people for good purposes, that his heart was good towards his red children. How then does it happen that his heart is changed?

Father. You have called upon us to fulfill the treaty of Greenville. In that treaty it was said that we should tell of any hostile intention towards one another. I now tell you that we have no information from any quarter that there was any design to hurt the people of the United States, except from yourself. You have told us that the thunder begins to roll.

Father. Your speech has overtaken us on our homeward march from Vincennes. We have heard it. We are not scared. We are going on towards that country that has been frequented by Tecumseh. We shall be able to know whether you or Tecumseh is correct, or whether other Indians are of the same mind with him. When we return we shall be able to tell whether Tecumseh has told the truth or not.

Now, Father, you hear what I have to say. You shall hear it well, what comes from me. You told us before we went to see you—twice you told us, that you were angry with us, because, while we had been sitting face to face and toes to toes, we had struck you and had said nothing about it. You now tell us that you sent a messenger after us and that we have insulted him, you and your Great Father This is twice you have told us, that you have been angry with us. We have looked for the cause, but could see none.

Father. We, the Miamis, are not a passionate people. We are not made angry so easily as it appears you are. Our hearts are as heavy as earth. Our minds are not easily irritated. We do not tell people we are angry for light causes. We are afraid that if we did, we would become contemptible in their eyes. We hope you will no more say you are angry with us, least you make yourself contemptible to your own people. We have told you we would not get angry for light causes. We have our eyes on our lands on the Wabash, with a strong determination to defend our rights against all aggressors, come from what quarter they may. When our best interests are invaded we will protect them to the last man of us, and be mad but once.

Father. Once more consider your children, the Miamis, and what they have said to you. You have now offered the war club to us. You have laid it at our feet, that, if we choose to pick it up, we might. We have refused to receive it from you. We hope this circumstance will prove to you that we have good hearts.

Father. I hope you will not be angry with us any more and we will not be angry with you."

In further reply to some remarks made by Mr. Dubois, the messenger of Gov. Harrison, Lapussia, said:

" If the Governor draws a line and leaves us out, he may strike us if he will, but if our rights are invaded from any quarter, we will die to a man, before we will relinquish them."

Other speeches were made by Silver Heels, Five Medals and Little Turtle in reply to Governor Harrison, none of which, however, were entirely satisfactory. At the risk of being deemed tedious, we will here insert the reply of Little Turtle, simply as a specimen of his earnest and simple style of speaking.

"Father. Your speech by Dubois, was communicated by him yesterday. Your children, the Miamis of Wabash, are all glad to hear what you have to say.

Father. You have asked whether we were prepared to take part with the Prophet, or to hold you fast by the hand. This question gives us to understand that some misunderstanding has taken place between you and some of our people. It appears also that you have made your intentions known to the Pottawatamies and other Indians, with respect to the Prophet. You have told them and us to leave him. These are things that have surprised us. The transaction that took place at Greenville is still fresh in our memories. At that place we told each other that we would be friends, doing all the good we could to each other, raising our children in peace and quietness. These are yet the sentiments of the Miamis.

Father. You have told us that you would draw a line—that your children should stand on one side, and you on the other. We, the Miamis, wish to be considered in the same light as we were at the Treaty of Greenville, holding fast to that treaty that united us as one people. These are also the sentiments of the Pottawatamies.

Father. Listen to what I say. It is our wish that you pay particular attention. We pray you not to bloody our ground if you can avoid it. Let the Prophet, in the first instance, be mildly requested to comply with your wishes, and avoid spilling of blood. The land on the Wabash is ours. We have not placed the Prophet there. On the contrary, we have endeavored to stop his going there. He must be considered as settling there without our leave.

Father. I must again repeat your saying, you must draw a line between your children and the Shawnee. We are not pleased at this, because we think you have no right to doubt our friendship towards you. I have not said much, but I think I have said enough at present. If my words are few, my meaning is great. I hope that you will pay particular attention to what I have said."

These speeches were delivered at Fort Wayne on the 4th of September, 1811, and are copied from manuscripts written at the time by John Shaw, Sub-Indian Agent, which were found among the papers of our late fellow-citizen, B. F. Stickney, Esq.

The battle of Tippecanoe was fought on the 7th of November, about two months after these speeches were made. Some time previous to this event, and while residing at the mouth of the Maumee, Peter Navarre was invited by John Songcraint to accompany him on a fur trading expedition to the west. They visited several tribes of Indians, among others the Prairie Pottawatamies, near Chicago, but did not purchase many furs. Navarre complained of their want of success, but Songcraint assured him they would supply themselves on their return home. After a month or more, they came to the Prophet's town, arriving there the same day that Gen. Harrison arrived with his army. Navarre was informed that their object was to make a treaty. He saw the chiefs leave the camp to meet the Governor, and listened to their remarks on their return. At an early hour he retired. At midnight he was awakened by the noise made by the Indians while picking their gun flints. He was about to rise for the purpose of ascertaining the cause, but was told by Songcraint if he did, that the Indians would kill him. He kept still, and in two hours afterwards, heard the firing and clash of the battle, some three miles distant from him. Learning of the result, the next morning, and finding the Indian town nearly evacuated, he left, with Songcraint, by the most feasible route, to avoid Harrison's soldiers, who he felt would shoot him or hang him, as a refugee in the British interest, should they arrest him.

Ells-kwa-ta-wa's power for evil over the western tribes had

been felt for years. As early as 1806 he visited the Wyandotts at Lower Sandusky and designated four of their best women as witches, whom he appointed men to slay at midnight. This fearful deed would have been consummated, but for the timely interference of Rev. Joseph Badger, missionary to the Wyandotts. As late as April, 1810, Governor Hull addresses the Wyandotts a speech on the folly of their belief in the delusions of the Prophet. "Consider," he says, "the consequences of such conduct. Let it once be proclaimed that the Crane and Leatherlips are witches, and any one has a right to murder them." Crane and Leatherlips were the head chiefs of the nation. The Prophet was a kind of uncivilized Joe Smith—full of low cunning, always ready with an incantation to justify his iniquity. What Tecumseh could not accomplish by persuasion and noble address, his brother would sometimes succeed in doing by trickery and conjuration. The tardy settlement of this valley from 1808 to 1811 is attributable in a great measure to the dread of encountering the confederated army of Tecumseh, which had been so long congregating at Tippecanoe. This was brought to a termination by the Battle of Tippecanoe, and peace, for a brief period, spread her white wings over the frontier.

Immigrants began to pour into this valley as soon as it was understood that the power of Tecumseh and the Prophet had been broken. The month before war was declared against Great Britain, there were sixty-seven white families settled upon the twelve mile square reserve, at the foot of the rapids. The most conspicuous man among the early settlers was Major Amos Spafford. He came to Ohio, in the employ of the Connecticut Land Company, towards the close of the last century, and settled at Cleveland. In 1810 he removed to this River to perform the duties of Collector of the Port of Miami, and Post Master. His first abstract of exports for the quarter ending June 30th, 1810, amounted to $5,640 85. The articles were twenty gallons of Bear's oil and a lot of skins and furs.

Major Spafford erected his dwelling on the plain in front, but a little above the elevated table of land, on which Fort Meigs was afterwards built. A little village grew up around him— and the settlers soon learned to regard him as their chief friénd and adviser. Another settlement sprang up about the same time on the spot where the village of Monclova stands. A saw and grist mill were erected there. These little hamlets were the only evidences of civilization between Lower Sandusky and Frenchtown or Monroe.

The intelligence that war was declared in 1812, was first communicated to the settlers of the valley by Peter Manor, the father of our fellow-townsman John J. Manor, Esq. He received it from a Delaware Chief by the name of Sac-a-manc, who with two of his tribe passed through the settlement on a marauding expedition to the interior of the State. The story told by Sac-a-manc was that war had been declared, but the British had not determined upon their plans for the campaign. "I," said the chief, "shall go to Owl Creek. I shall kill some of the Longknives before I come back, and will show you some of their scalps. In ten days after I get back, all the hostile tribes will hold a council at Malden, and very soon after that we shall come to this place and kill all the Yankees. You, Manor, are a good Frenchman and must not tell them what I say." Sac-a-manc returned after an absence of six days, and showed Manor three scalps which he said were those of a family he had murdered on Owl Creek. He repeated to Manor in confidence that it was the intention of the Indians to come to the valley in force sufficient to massacre the American settlers. This intelligence Manor communicated to Major Spafford, accompanied with advice to leave the valley immediately. The Major laughed, and dismissed the subject with some remark expressive of incredulity, and Manor left him with the promise that should he learn of any further cause for alarm he would let him know. Three days after this conversation a man by the name of Miller, who had lived many years with the Ottawas, and who was well known to Major Spafford, entered his house in breathless haste, and told him that at no greater distance than Monclova, there was a band of fifty Pottawatamies. They were on the march from their country on the St. Josephs, to join the hostile Indians at Malden, and take part in the council spoken of by Sac-a-manc. They had plundered and set fire to the dwellings and mills at Monclova, and would soon be on their march for the foot of the rapids. But little time was left to escape. The major with his family, and the few settlers that had remained in the valley, hastened immediately to the river, where they dislodged and launched a large barge, in which some officers had descended the river from Fort Wayne, the year before. Raising a square sail composed of a bed blanket, they were enabled by dint of hard rowing and a favorable breeze, to round the point and get under cover of old Fort Miami, just as the Indians made their appearance on the bank, where Maumee City is built, and before they passed Eagle Point they saw the flames ascending from the homes they had just deserted. This little band of fugitives, favored with fair winds, made a safe passage to the Quaker Settlement at Milan, where they remained until after the war. Manor says they were panic-struck and left their horses, cattle, and most of their household goods, which were taken away by the Indians, who completed their work by burning every dwelling belonging to an American in that part of the valley. This accomplished, they pursued their march to Malden, attended the Council, and true to the appointment of Sac-a-manc some two hundred of the hostile Indians afterwards came to the rapids, and finished so much of the work of destruction as was left undone by the Pottawatamies.

All this occurred immediately after Gen. Hull's march from Dayton to Detroit, and before the surrender of the latter place to the British. Gen. Hull's army was raised for the avowed purpose of protecting the frontier from Indian depredations—though with the expectation that war would be declared against

Great Britain, in a short time. Our fellow-citizen Gen. John
E. Hunt was one of Gen. Hull's military family, while on the
march from Dayton to Detroit. The army was encamped several weeks at Urbana, awaiting the arrival of the 4th United
States Regiment, then on its march from Vincennes to join
them. This was a regiment composed of sailors and others
who, by reason of the embargo, had been thrown out of employ, and were selected, with special regard to their fitness for
military service, by Col. Boyd, under whom they fought with
great gallantry at Tippecanoe. Hull's troops were encamped
upon a wooded knoll. They had sprung a beautiful arch of
evergreens over the road, midway up the ascent into the encampment, on which was inscribed in large letters, the words
" Tippecanoe Glory." Under this arch the 4th Regiment
marched into camp. Their appearance, with their bucket caps
and cartridge boxes, every man in perfect drill, has been described as very imposing. They were under command of Lieutenant Colonel Miller.

The march from Urbana was long and tedious. The country
for most of the distance, being entirely new, the troops were
obliged to cut the road over which they travelled. It was a
bright June morning when they emerged from the wilderness
upon the bank of the Maumee, which they struck at the head
of a large flat, about five miles above Perrysburg. There they
encamped for a day and then marched down to the flat, below
Miami, at which point the ladies, invalids, some of the stores,
and the private papers of Gen. Hull were placed on board the
little schooner Miami, which immediately sailed for Detroit.

The army resumed its march, and between Maumee and River Raisin received intelligence that war had been declared—
too late, alas! to recall the vessel which fell into the hands of
the enemy at Malden. Vain of his army and proud of display-
ing it, Gen. Hull remained a day at River Raisin, for no other
purpose, apparently, than to give the inhabitants an opportunity
of witnessing the evolutions of his soldiers. Between River

Raisin and Huron River, many of the Indians, who were afterwards allied with the British, came up with the army and be-
sought Gen. Hull to remove their women and children beyond
the reach of danger, and to accept their services during the
war. Tish-kwa-gwon, Otussa and Mesh-ke-ma were among
the number. Prohibited by his orders from government, from
employing Indians in the service, all that Gen. Hull could do,
was to advise them to abstain from any participation in the
conflict. The Indians argued the impossibility of neutrality,
but Hull was pertinacious for its observance, and they left him
filled with indignation at the cool reception he had given them.
While encamped at Huron River, the army saw British armed
vessels off the mouth of Detroit River, and other warlike preparations. Here they made their first preparations for an attack,
which, at one time, during the night, they supposed had been
commenced.

Gen. Hull marched with his army into Canada, but from
some cause, never fully understood, but supposed by many to
have been imbecility, remained for six weeks encamped at
Sandwich, on any day of which period, he might have captured
Malden and effected the military occupation of the Province.
While there he sent out several expeditions against the enemy,
and two to effect a union with Col. Brush who had arrived at
River Raisin, with four or five hundred head of cattle for the
use of the army. The last of these expeditions was under
command of Col. Miller, who met the British and Indians at
Monguagua and effected a passage through their ranks. Me-
dor Coutture, Esq., of Monroe, says that previous to the arrival
of Col. Brush at Raisin, he had enlisted as a private in the
Cavalry under Capt. Richard Smith, and those who lived at
River Raisin, were under the command of Cornet Isaac Lee.
They performed no other service for some time after their organization, than that of escorting the United States mail from
Raisin to Detroit, but on the occasion of the battle of Mongua-
gua, they marched to the scene of action and participated in

the conflict, contributing in no small degree to the achievment of Miller's victory. After this was over, and with the mail under their escort, while on their return to Raisin, they fell into an ambush in the marsh at Brownstown. The Indians wounded Louis Jacob, but killed none. An instance of coolness is related of Achan Leboo, one of the French soldiers whose canteen was tapped by a bullet. "By George," said he, raising the vessel to his mouth "before they get my whiskey, I will drink it."

Gen. Dearborn having entered into an armistice at the lower end of the Lake, Gen. Brock hastened with his army to Detroit. Gen. Hull re-crossed the river, when he heard of his approach, and garrisoned Fort Detroit. Brock demanded a surrender, which was declined, and bombardment and cannonading commenced. Gen. Hunt says, that balls and bombs came against the Fort with great regularity, but there were no indications of a surrender until a thirty-two pound shot came, which struck Lieut. Hanks, Major Sibley and Dr. Reynolds, killing them instantly and severely wounding Dr. Blood. At the time this occurred Gen. Hunt was standing near the unfortunate men, and where he could also see the effect which their loss produced upon Gen. Hull. He says, that he saw the old man's lips tremble, and the tobacco juice ran from his mouth upon his bosom. When the next shot came he ran up the white flag.

Peter Navarre joined Hull's army on the Maumee, went to Detroit, and then returned to Raisin, where he enlisted in Col. Anderson's Regiment. He was at Raisin when the British Captain, Elliott, accompanied by a Frenchman and a Wyandot, came with a flag, to inform Col. Brush, and the troops at Raisin, that they were included in the surrender of Hull. Lieutenant Coutture, officer of the day, blindfolded Elliott and led him into the Guard House. Upon learning his errand, Brush indignantly refused to comply with the terms of the surrender, and gave orders to Coutture to place Elliott under arrest. He was locked in the Guard House. Brush hastily packed up the property in the Fort and retreated, taking with him the cattle, he had brought, leaving orders for the release of Elliott the next morning, which were obeyed. Elliott was very angry and sent immediately to Tecumseh, who at the head of a band of Indians came to Raisin for the purpose of pursuing Brush, but finding it too late, he abandoned the enterprise in disgust. Navarre and his four brothers acknowledged the terms of the surrender, and were permitted to depart on parole.

Some weeks previous to the surrender of Detroit, a large force of hostile Indians, by a simultaneous movement, had invested Forts Wayne and Harrison, and held them in siege. Our late esteemed fellow-citizen, Major B. F. Stickney, had been appointed Indian Agent by President Madison, and was at Fort Wayne during the siege. Having accidentally learned, before the siege was commenced, that the Indians were preparing for it, he dispatched a messenger to Cincinnati with the request that relief should be sent to the forts as soon as possible. Gen. Harrison had just been appointed by the State of Kentucky to the command of her troops, and set out upon the march as soon as he had received Stickney's message. In the meantime the Indians established lines of guard around Fort Wayne, and opened upon it an incessant fire of small arms. For the purpose of inducing the people in the fort to believe that they were provided with cannon, they scooped out logs and fastened them together, so as to form rude wooden guns, which they charged with powder and fired, making a great deal of noise, and raising a great deal of dust, without effecting their object. There were less than one hundred people in the fort, and from six to eight hundred Indians surrounding it. It was a small, frail stockade, which could not have withstood the attack of regular troops six hours. The danger of a capture was very imminent, and daily growing more so as the siege progressed. Uncertain as to the success of the messenger who was sent to Cincinnati, the little garrison kept vigilant watch of the enemy, and used no more ammunition than was necessary to keep the Indians away from the pickets, while they awaited not without uncertainty, but yet without fear the event of the siege. Gen. Harrison, anxious to relieve the suspense which he felt must affect the inmates of the besieged garrison, and also to inspire them with fresh courage, selected from his troops a young officer, whom he charged with the difficult and dangerous service of penetrating the wilderness to the fort, and running the Indian line of guard to the sally port. The person selected was Major William Oliver. He was accompanied by four Shawanese. After a march of sixty miles they came near the outposts of the enemy. Oliver was in Indian costume. It was broad mid-day. Warily did they examine every pass and scan every thicket until they came within sight of the pickets. Then the time for timidity had passed, and all seemed to depend upon the strength and activity of the legs. They broke into a fleet run—all feeling that it was to be a race for life. They reached the fort, without being discovered, and Oliver remained there until the siege was brought to a close. His assurance that aid was near, renewed the zeal with which the inmates of the fort engaged in its defence. Gen. Harrison's army arrived on the 10th of September. The Indians fled at its approach, filling the wilderness around with their whoops and yells.

The massacre of Chicago and the surrender of Detroit exposed the entire frontier to the enemy, except so much of it as was protected by Forts Wayne and Harrison, both of which had almost miraculously escaped the investments to which they had been subjected. The enemy were not slow to avail themselves of their supposed advantages. News that Fort Wayne had been relieved did not reach Detroit before Hull's surrender, and as a consequence, the first act of Gen. Brock was to detach from his troops and Indians, six hundred of each, to reinforce the besiegers of Fort Wayne. Manor says that the first intimation of Hull's surrender was given to the French settlers at the foot of the rapids, by a party of sixty or seventy Delawares, who arrived there in advance of the main body of the army, on the march to Fort Wayne. He says that he, with some of his neighbors, was standing in front of Beaugrand's store at Maumee, when the Indians came out of the woods— that they drew up in line, and each put his gun to his shoulder and aimed, as if to fire, at the little group of settlers. Beaugrand came out and waved a white handkerchief. They dropped their muskets and approached the store, on a run. They remained but a few minutes. An hour after their departure, about one hundred British soldiers and as many Pottawatamies and Wyandotts came up. Their first enquiry was for guides. Manor, from prudential motives, was seized with sudden and severe lameness. It would not do. The officer in command pressed him into service as a guide, and lame as he seemed, he was compelled to conduct this company to the head of the rapids. Here his lameness increased so much, that it disqualified him for further travel, and his persecutors dismissed him. He set out on his return home. When about half way, he met a band of Pottawatamies, who took him prisoner, and demanded where he was going. He told them he had been ordered back to procure forage for the cattle and horses. They let him go. At the foot of Presque Isle Hill, he met Col. Elliott, the officer in command of the detachment, and the remainder of the troops and Indians composing it. Elliott examined him closely, and on learning that he had been employed as a guide, and had been discharged for lameness and incompetency, he bestowed upon him a curse or two, and permitted him to go on his way rejoicing. He proceeded to Beaugrand's. Finding that the country was getting too hot for him, and sympathizing with the American cause, he left the rapids to join his family, which had previously removed to the dwelling of Robert Navarre at the mouth of the river. At Swan Creek, he came suddenly upon two British vessels. The officer in command, not satisfied with his account of himself, took him prisoner, and confined him under hatches. He staid there until Beaugrand could be informed

4

of his condition, and upon his representation that Manor was a tory, he was released, and joined his family without further impediment.

Before Gen. Harrison left Fort Wayne, he was joined by Brigadier Gen. Winchester of the regular service. He took command of the regulars, and a sufficient number of volunteers to make up an army of 1700, and marched down the Maumee. Near Defiance he discovered the advance guard of the British army, which had proceeded thus far on their march to reinforce the Indians. Peter Navarre had accompanied the British as a guide on this expedition. At Turkey Foot he found an opportunity to leave them, and hastening on in advance, to inform the beleaguered garrison, had met and apprised Winchester of their approach, some hours before they came in sight, and then returned to the British. Winchester arranged his lines, so as to make a great show of numbers, and when the British beheld them approaching, with the apparent determination to engage in instant conflict, they beat a hurried retreat without stoppages until they reached Malden. Gen. Winchester remained with his army at Defiance, and built the stockade fort known as Camp Winchester.

The left wing of the army soon marched from Camp Winchester, ten miles below Defiance, to Camp No. 3, where they remained nearly three months. The sufferings of the soldiers from sickness, cold and starvation during this period were horrible, upwards of three hundred were daily upon the sick list. Typhus fever, in its most malignant form, daily swept five or six into the grave. Many were so destitute of shoes and clothing, that they would have frozen on any march from their quarters. Provisions soon began to disappear. The men were allowed but half rations. At length the flour gave out entirely, and poor beef, and the roots of hickory saplings roasted, became the only means of subsistence. The other wing of the army was encamped at Upper Sandusky, more than one hundred miles distant, and only accessible by a march through the pathless wilderness. Gen. Winchester had received orders from Gen. Harrison, to advance to the foot of the rapids as soon as he had accumulated twenty days' provisions, and commence building huts there, to induce the enemy to believe he was going into winter quarters. This march was commenced on the 30th December.

In the meantime, Manor, finding his family safe, planned a little expedition on his own account which partook largely of the romance that had thus far attended him through the war. He had several friends among the French residing at River Raisin, whom he was desirous of removing to the mouth of Maumee. Accordingly on the night of the 18th January, with his eldest son for company, he started for Frenchtown, on a rude sled drawn by a pony. The night was clear and beautiful, the weather extremely cold, and the ice of the lake covered with a heavy incrusted snow. He approached Frenchtown in a few hours, and hearing the sound of musketry, left his horse with his boy and hastened to the scene of action. It was the brilliant attack and victory of Major Lewis. Manor sent some female friends, with his son, back to Navarres, and remained himself to share the fortune of the American army, now advancing to reinforce Major Lewis. The history of the bloody massacre of the Raisin has never been correctly published. Medor Coutture and Peter Navarre, both eye witnesses and actors, unite in the correctness of the following details, taken from their own mouths.

After Navarre and his four brothers left the Raisin on parole, they returned to the mouth of the Maumee, and when Colonels Lewis and Allen advanced to Presque Isle, from Camp No. 3, and were importuned to march to the relief of the settlers at Frenchtown, they were employed as their guides. Coutture, also on parole, remained at Frenchtown. Lewis and Allen marched with their troops on the ice from Presque Isle to the site of the old dock on River Raisin, near Monroe. The British and Indians were on the north bank of the river, encamped upon grounds on which the dwelling of Coutture's parents stood. They had a six-pounder which they discharged repeatedly without effect. The Americans charged upon them, and drove them from their position, and continued the battle from about three o'clock until dark. They were left in possession of the field. This was the 18th day of January. Next day, Col. Wells, with a battalion of two hundred men, arrived, and encamped on the Reaume farm, some distance from the camp of Lewis and Allen. Gen. Winchester, accompanied by his aid, Capt. Wolverton, arrived on the 20th, and established his head quarters at the house of Col. Francis Navarre, a mile distant from either of the camps, and on the opposite side of the river. He visited the camp of Lewis and Allen on the 20th, and at that time was introduced to the family of Mr. Coutture, senior, after which he returned to his quarters at Col. Navarre's.

On the morning of the 21st, Peter Navarre and his four brothers, by Winchester's request, went on a scouting expedition towards the mouth of Detroit River. They saw on the ice, at a great distance, a solitary man approaching them on a run. He proved to be Joseph Bordeau, since the father-in-law of Peter Navarre, who was making his escape from Malden, where he had been held as a prisoner.

"My lad," said he, addressing Peter, "the Americans will be attacked by the whole British army to-night. I know it."

The brothers conducted Bordeau to Winchester, and he told him the same. A Frenchman, who proved to have been in the British interest, by the name of Jocko Lasalle, stood by, and lulled the fears of the unsuspecting General, by asserting in the most positive language, that it must be a mistake. Winchester dismissed the scouts with a laugh, but made no preparation to meet the threatened danger. Another scout came in during the afternoon, with intelligence confirmatory of that given by Bordeau, but Winchester remained incredulous.

In the evening, Coutture accompanied Adjutant McCalley on a visit to Dr. Austin, Surgeon of the 2d Regiment, who was sick of consumption. They remained with him until about nine o'clock, when Coutture suggested they had better return, as they were without the countersign. McCalley replied that he had it. It was a dim starlight night. On their return to camp, they passed a man walking hastily. Coutture enquired, "What is the matter? You are in a hurry."

"Yes," he replied. "It is time to be in a hurry."

"Why so?" rejoined Coutture.

"The British and Indians, in full force, are at Stony Creek, only four miles distant."

This man, whose name was John La Bresh, fled. McCalley and Coutture went on to the camp. In the parlor of the house were seated Colonels Lewis, Allen, Major Madison and others engaged in conversation. Coutture leaned upon the chair of Major Garrard.

"Medor," enquired the Major, "what news do you bring?"

"Very bad news, Major," replied Coutture. "The British and Indians, in full force, are within four miles of us."

The officers started to their feet simultaneously, and Garrard said: "Then we must prepare to meet them;" and, in company with several others, he went out and stationed the picket guard around the camp.

McCalley, Ensign Baker, and Major William O. Butler slept crosswise on one bed that night. A little before daylight, Coutture kicked the drummer, who was lying beside the fire-place, and told him to beat the reveille. While he was playing the tune called "Three Camps," the British opened their fire with all their artillery, consisting of six field pieces and mortars. Navarre and his brothers had taken possession of an old horse-mill a short distance from the camp, where they contrived to do good service with their rifles, during the engagement.

The luckless commander, aroused by the firing, strove to join his army, from which he was separated by the river and nearly a mile of distance. Mounting Col. Navarre's horse, he rode, heedlessly, in what he supposed to be the direction of the camp, but had not gone far before he fell into the hands of Jack Brandy, an Indian belonging to Round Head's band, by whom, after being divested of nearly all his clothing, he was conducted, in a half frozen condition, to Proctor. Proctor persuaded Jack to surrender the General to him and restore his clothing. Until the capture of Gen. Winchester, the Americans had maintained a successful defence. At one time, Proctor had ordered the firing to cease, with a view to suspend hostilities, but with Winchester for a prisoner, he dictated his own terms of capitulation. Winchester sent his aid, with peremptory orders, to Major Madison, the officer left in command, to surrender, which were as peremptorily declined. He then went to Madison, in charge of an Indian, and told him, that his own life and the safety of the army depended upon his prompt and unconditional surrender. Madison again declined, but finally agreed to do so, upon condition that all private property should be respected ; that sleds should be provided next morning to remove the sick and wounded to Malden ; that in the meantime they should be protected by a guard, and that their side-arms should be restored to them on their arrival at Malden, to which Proctor agreed. The heaviest loss of our army in the battle fell upon the battalion of Col. Wells, which, in attempting to join Col. Lewis' troops, got into confusion and lost two hundred men, who were cut to pieces. Had they encamped with Col. Lewis, instead of occupying the Reaume farm, upon their arrival, the American arms would probably have been victorious.

Peter Navarre and his brothers, still in possession of the old horse-mill, now that the army had surrendered, found themselves in the dilemma of prisoners who had violated their parole.

"What shall we do ?" enquired Robert, clasping his throat significantly. "If we are captured, we shall be hung."

"Let's run," replied Peter. "Better die by a bullet than a rope." And suiting the action to the word, the brothers showed their enemies a clean pair of heels. With Indians in hot pursuit, and balls whistling around them like hail, they meandered through the marsh grass, and ran far out upon the lake, and effected their escape. Before evening they went to Presque Isle, and during the night, Robert, the elder brother, returned stealthily, to the scene of battle.

Medor Coutture, with two Frenchman by the names of Brineau and Beaugrand, and Dr. Bower and Hunter, was left in charge of the Hospital, a house near by, belonging to John Jerome. There were forty-five wounded in the house:—among others, Major Madison and Capt. Hart, a brother-in-law of Hon. Henry Clay. Looking in the direction of Malden, next morning, Coutture saw, instead of the promised sleds, about three hundred Indians approaching.

"Capt. Hart," said he, entering the apartment of the wounded officer, "we are all gone. The Indians are coming instead of the sleds."

Soon after, the work of massacre commenced in earnest. The savages tomahawked, scalped and plundered the wounded without mercy, and thus perished some of the most brilliant young men of Kentucky. Before life had fairly left the mangled bodies of the unfortunate victims, the buildings were fired, and the dead and dying were consumed together. Coutture and Doctor Bower were stripped and tied by a band of Chippewas, and stood near the blazing ruins, in momentary expectation of death. An old Ottawa Chief, by the name of Wau-gon, who had been a friend of Coutture before the war, was reeling with drunkenness in the road near by. Coutture beckoned to him. He came to him, recognized him, and comprehending the horrors of his condition, put his finger in his mouth and gave a shrill whistle. Immediately, several Indians came running to the spot.

"Take care of him," said Wau-gon, pointing to Coutture. "Give him his clothes. He is my son. His father lies dead in the yard, and I am now his father. Don't harm him." He gave Coutture the name of Sa-gua-na, which signified Be brave, and Coutture understanding that he was now safe, interceded, and not unsuccessfully, with his Indian father for the life of Dr. Bower, and that gentleman was, not many years ago, a Senator from Missouri. Wau-gon took him to Detroit, and afterwards Coutture saw him on their march to the Thames.

Jack Brandy, while conveying Winchester as his prisoner to Proctor's camp, captured Whitmore Knaggs, the old Potta-watamie Agent, and father of George and James Knaggs of this valley. Sometime before the war, Knaggs had caused Jack to be flogged for some offence, and ascertaining who had taken him, supposed as a matter of course that he would be slain. Jack re-assured him with promises of safety. Before they arrived at the camp, they were met by a band of Potta-watamies, who, with upraised tomahawks, rushed towards Knaggs. Jack stepped between them and his prisoner, told them they must kill him before they killed Knaggs, and thus saved him from massacre.

This same Jack Brandy, a few days before the massacre of Raisin, in conversation with Harry Hunt of Detroit, told him, that if occasion ever offered, he would be kind to the Yan-kees, and bring any that might fall into his hands, to Detroit without injury. This promise he so far fulfilled, as to drag from the buildings, at the massacre, a large Kentuckian by the name of John Green, who had been wounded in the engage-ment. Wrapping him carefully in his blanket, he laid him in the bottom of his carryall, and started on a trot for Detroit. The next morning, Hunt saw Jack drive up in front of the town, and with one or two friends went to see him.

" Well, Jack," he enquired, " have you brought us some venison to-day ? "

" Yes, Harry Hunt," replied the Indian, throwing the blan-ket off his captive. " Good Yankee venison. There, Harry Hunt," he continued, as soon as Hunt discovered that the prisoner was one of the Raisin captives. "I told you Jack Brandy cannot lie."

Mr. Hunt purchased the liberty of Green, took him to his house, and afterwards restored him to his friends, who, supposing he was slain, enlisted under Harrison to avenge his death.

Sometime before the close of the war, Harry Hunt bought a large, dapple grey horse, which was stolen soon after, by a band of Pottawatamies. On entering his store, a day or two afterwards, Hunt encountered Jack Brandy, who, observing the seriousness of his countenance, enquired as to the cause. On being informed, Jack simply replied, "May be me get him again," and mounted his pony and started in pursuit. He soon struck the trail of the Pottawatamies, and came up with them two days afterwards. He camped with them on the night of his arrival, and told them he had a special mission to the Indians near Chicago, which had an important bearing upon the war. This pleased his entertainers, and they told him about the fine horse they had got. Jack, upon the plea of urgent business, bantered them for a trade, promising, if on trial, the horse proved to be good, to pay the difference between him and his pony. At daylight, the horse with his saddle and bridle, was brought up for Jack to prove. He bestrode him, rode a short distance in the direction of Chicago, struck into the woods, and that was the last his Indian friends saw of him. The next day he rode into Detroit at top speed, and surrendering the horse to his owner, repeated most emphatically :

"There, Harry Hunt, I tell you once more, Jack Brandy cannot lie."

The horse was afterwards sold to Proctor for one hundred guineas, and on him, that infamous coward made his escape at the Thames.

Otussa, already named as the son of Pontiac, captured Capt. Baker of the 17th Infantry, at the battle of River Raisin. On his return to Detroit with his prisoner, accompanied by his son Wa-se-on-quet, he encamped the first night at Huron River.

5

He ordered his son to make a fire. The young man asked why the Yankee dog could not do it.

"My son," answered Otussa, "such language is wrong. This prisoner is a chief among his own people. We must treat him as we would wish to be treated under like circumstances."

Otussa obeyed this golden rule, took the best of care of his prisoner, bought tea, butter, sugar, and other expensive luxuries for him. Baker was sent to Quebec, but exchanged in time to join Harrison's army and take part in the battle of the Thames. The day after the return of the army from the Thames to Detroit, a band of Indians with a white flag, was seen to emerge from the wilderness in rear of the town. Harrison ordered Capt. Baker to treat with them. He approached them, and recognized in their leader his old captor and friend Otussa. The meeting between them was highly affecting. Baker did not fail to repay, fourfold, the favor which had been bestowed upon him by the noble Indian.

On the retreat of the Indians from the engagement of the 18th January, with Capt. Lewis, some of them entered the cabin of Achan Leboo, an old Frenchman, living upon Sandy Creek. They killed Leboo and his son-in-law John Solo. Two children, Alexis and Geneveive, the eldest only fourteen, crept between the beds, where they remained all night without discovery, and by running barefoot, the next day, a mile or more over frozen ground, escaped with their lives.

The fate of Capt. Nathaniel Hart, as detailed by Capt. Coutture, is one of the most affecting incidents connected with the massacre. Hart had been wounded in the calf of his leg. When the Indians came to the hospital, the morning after the battle, a Pottawatamie chief, by the name of Os-a-med, threw his blanket over the Captain, and lifted him upon his pony. Coutture, who knew Os-a-med, promised him a reward to take good care of Captain Hart. Designing to do so, Os-a-med started with his prisoner for Detroit, on an old blind trail, but had proceeded but a short distance, before Capt. Hart fell from his saddle, with a bullet in his brain, fired by a Chippewa. The Indians stripped and scalped him, leaving his body to become a prey to the wolves. A mile beyond the spot where Hart fell, a young man by the name of Henry Shovin, son of one of the settlers, lay dead in the road. In the night, after the Indians had departed, Shovin, the father, accompanied by Coutture, went after the body of the young man, which they brought to Shovin's house, directly in front of which lay the body of Capt. Hart. They hid young Shovin's body in the cellar, and first covering that of Capt. Hart, with bark, they buried it in the hollow made by the roots of a fallen tree.

As soon after the massacre of the Raisin as safety would permit, Gen. Harrison advanced from his camp on Portage River to the foot of the rapids, and built Fort Meigs, which was the only fort on the frontier, in the Spring of 1813, at all prepared to resist an attack of the enemy. It was anticipated that an attack would be made as soon as the lake broke up in the Spring. It was, therefore, important that the army, garrisoned at Fort Meigs, should be re-enforced as soon as possible, as the fall of that post would expose the whole frontier to fire and massacre.

Navarre and his brothers were employed as scouts, by Harrison, as soon as Fort Meigs was completed. When the Indians first made their appearance, Navarre discovered them crossing the river, at the foot of the large island. On reporting this to Harrison, he gave him three letters, one to Lower Sandusky —one to Upper Sandusky, and a third to Governor Meigs, at Urbana. Navarre departed, and at the close of the fifth day handed the message to Gov. Meigs. Meigs sent messengers in all directions for volunteers. Two days afterwards, Col. Duncan McArthur left Urbana at the head of eighteen hundred men, to re-enforce Gen. Harrison. At Fort Findley, they were met by a messenger from Harrison, with intelligence of the successful repulse of the British and McArthur's troops disbanded.

Two regiments, under command of Gen. Green Clay, marched for the exposed fortress, from Kentucky, early in April, over the route traversed by Gen. Winchester. At St. Mary's block-house, Gen. Clay divided the brigade, sending Col. Dudley's regiment across to the Auglaize River, and descending the St. Mary's himself, at the head of Col. Boswell's troops, intending to unite the two regiments at Defiance. While this march was in progress, the enemy made their appearance on the bank of the river opposite the fort, which, as none of the new levies had arrived, was very indifferently manned by less than one thousand men. In this exigency, Gen. Harrison sent Major Oliver, as an express, to Gen. Clay, with orders to hasten his march with the Kentucky reinforcements. Oliver, accompanied by one Indian and one white man, performed this hazardous service successfully, having found Gen. Clay at Fort Winchester.

On the night of the next day after Oliver left Fort Meigs, Col. Dudley sent Leslie Combs as an express to Fort Meigs to inform Gen. Harrison of his advance, and to receive his orders. Combs, accompanied by four whites, and Black-Fish, a young Shawnee warrior, descended the river in a pirogue without accident, but did not arrive in sight of the Fort until the morning of the next day had far advanced. He was discovered by the Indians, after he had arrived in sight of the beleaguered garrison, fired at, and one of his men killed, and being unable to effect an entrance, he left his pirogue, and with much difficulty and suffering, succeeded in re-joining his regiment two days afterwards. Oliver and Trimble were more successful. They entered the fort at a late hour the night before the sortie, bringing with them the welcome intelligence that Gen. Clay's reinforcement was within a few miles.

At this time, the enemy had poured an incessant fire upon the fort for four days, during which time, they had killed but one man. Foreseeing that some time would elapse before Clay's reinforcement would come up, Gen. Harrison had caused a grand traverse of earth, twenty feet high, to be thrown up for a distance of three hundred yards, through the centre of the fort. The British, in the mean time, were erecting their batteries on the opposite side of the river, and the work upon the traverse was hid from their view by the tents which were pitched in front of it.

On the morning of the 1st of May, before Proctor opened his batteries upon the fort, it is said he reconnoitered the American camp with his spy-glass, and while thus employed, much to his astonishment, he saw the tents struck, and in a few minutes afterwards, the tops of the poles which supported them, appearing above a solid embankment of earth, which covered and protected everything within range of his guns. Among the thousand and one stories told of his conduct, when he made this discovery, the remarks that it is said he made to his men, are not the least probable.

" Boys," said he, " we will commence the fire, but I despair of success. Men who can perform such a mountain of labor, will never be taken alive."

Three days afterwards, finding he had made but little impression upon the fort, and that all his balls were caught in the earth-work, he sent Major Chambers to the fort to demand a surrender. Harrison's reply was worthy of his fame :

" Tell Gen. Proctor," said he, " if he takes this fort, it will be under circumstances that will do him more honor than a thousand surrenders."

Firing and bombardment were renewed, and continued with unabated fury, until Gen. Clay's army made their appearance on the margin of the river, a mile above the batteries. Col. Dudley's regiment had received orders from Gen. Harrison to land at that place, and make a rapid assault upon the British batteries, capture them, spike their guns, and then withdraw under the bank of the river, leaving the discomfited enemy on the plain above, exposed to the fire of the guns of the fort. By a simultaneous movement, Col. Miller was to march from the fort, at the head of four hundred men, and dislodge the batteries which had been erected on the south side of the river. Both expeditions were successful. Miller's attack was one of the most brilliant achievements of the war. Dudley's would not have been a whit behind it, had his men obeyed the orders of the commanding General. The batteries were taken, the guns partly spiked, and the enemy driven from the ravine they had occupied, in range of the guns from the fort, upon the upland; but Dudley's troops, fired with the ardor of success, and eager to improve this opportunity to retaliate upon the enemy for the horrible Massacre at Raisin, instead of withdrawing under the bank, pursued their retreating foe for several miles into the wilderness. A large body of Indians, on their march from Malden to reinforce the British, came up while our troops were thus engaged, and comprehending the precise state of affairs, formed an ambush, into which the unsuspecting Kentuckians were decoyed, surrounded, and most inhumanly butchered,—only one hundred and forty, of eight hundred, escaping to tell the tale. Col. Dudley himself was among the slain.

Would to God, for the honor of our common humanity, that there were no more distressing details connected with this dreadful slaughter. Alas! for the boasted civilization—alas! for the chivalric spirit of Britain,—the unprecedented violation of all the rules of honorable warfare, and the horrible cruelties practiced at River Raisin and Fort Meigs, have fixed a stigma upon each, as damning as it is ineffaceable. Upon the surrender of our troops, one by one, as they arrived at the batteries, they were marched in single file, down to the British head-quarters, at old Fort Miami, there, soon to be followed by the Indians, their squaws, and their boys, and by them, plundered,— and if not tomahawked or shot, subjected to every species of insult and abuse. Capt. Leslie Combs, one of the prisoners, says that the Indians enfiladed the entrance to the fort, and tomahawked or shot such of the prisoners as were not able, by running the lines, to reach the interior in safety. The ditch was filled with Americans, who had been thus dispatched in sight of the butcher Proctor, and his officers. Soon after the prisoners, who had run this gauntlet, were in the fort, the Indians transferred their horrid sport to that arena, where, after slaughtering as many as they pleased, indiscriminately, they were making preparations to bring the tragedy to a speedy close, by shooting those that remained altogether, when a noble looking Indian entered hurriedly into their midst, drew his sword, and made a short but indignant speech. This was the great chief Tecumseh, who, until that moment, had been a stranger to the doings of his men. The work of murder, from that moment, ceased; though a bloody villain, who, but a few moments before, had struck his tomahawk into the skulls of four persons, showed such signs of disobedience, that Tecumseh threatened him with instant death, unless he desisted.

At dark the prisoners were marched to the mouth of Swan Creek, and confined under hatches on a brig and schooner, with nothing but the bare plank for a bed, and without food or surgical attention. In this condition they were taken to Malden, where, after a short period of confinement, they were liberated upon parole, and sent across the Lake in an open boat, to the mouth of Huron River, fifty miles distant from the nearest settlement in Ohio.

After the attack upon Fort Stephenson, in July, the British and Indians made no further aggressions, but remained in quarters at Detroit, like our own army, anxiously awaiting the result of the demonstrations progressing in another quarter. On the 8th of September, Navarre and one brother were sent to Com. Perry, then at Put-in-Bay, with orders to engage the British fleet as soon as possible. They arrived on the 9th, gave Perry the letter, were favored with a review of the seamen and marines, and returned to Fort Seneca the same night. The battle of Erie was fought next day, and the battle of the Thames soon followed. Navarre and his brothers were advance scouts on Col. Johnson's march from Fort Meigs to the Thames.

With this last action, the war in the northwest was brought to a glorious termination. Gen. Harrison entered into an armistice with the hostile Indians, and went, with some of his troops, to the Niagara frontier. The second treaty of Greenville took place soon after, at which Major Stickney, as Indian Agent, had seven thousand Indians to govern and feed. The treaty was effected after a meeting of two month's duration. The Indians renewed their fealty to the United States, and departed to their old settlements. From this time, until peace was declared, they were dependant upon our Government for support —for the reason, that they could not, without liability to exposure to our troops, go on their usual hunting expeditions. During the last year of the war, Major Stickney disbursed, for provisions alone, over three hundred thousand dollars. The condition of this frontier, at this period, is thus described by Major Stickney :

" The British authorities saw they might possibly make something out of predatory incursions by the Indians upon the partially protected frontier, as they had much the largest number of Indians who adhered to them. The Indians committed some depredations upon the scattered settlements. This produced a very uneasy state of mind among the inhabitants of Ohio and Indiana. Some hundreds of families broke and run. In this state of things, Gen. Harrison ordered the two principal Indian Agents, John Johnson, Esq., and myself, to head-quarters, at Cincinnati, to consult upon the ways and means of protecting the frontier. We made a written report to the General, the substance of which was, that as the Indians had their settlements scattered along the frontier, to confine them there, by feeding them daily, at their proper places of residence and no other, and to inform them that they must be responsible for the safety of the frontier ; that if they suffered the British Indians to kill the white people over their heads, the white people would retaliate by killing them, as often as opportunity offered. This answered a tolerable protection ; but the frontier inhabitants were yet in a very feverish state—hundreds fled--the friendly Indians were great objects of fear—the Agents, who doing all they could to protect them, were suspected of intentions to let the Indians loose, and were thus placed between two fires. The Indians grew impatient of restraint and made several efforts to escape, which were thwarted by the vigilance of the Agents."

Perhaps no frontier settlers suffered more from the war than those who dwelt in this valley. They lost their all. First, the British and Indians burned their houses, mills and furniture, and stole their cattle and horses before the arrival of the American troops. When they came, being out of provisions, they ravaged their cornfields, and left nothing that had escaped the plunder of the enemy. The amount of losses, sustained by eleven settlers at the foot of the rapids, exceeded $5,000. A small part of this amount was afterwards provided for by our Government, to cover the losses occasioned by our army.

On their return to the valley, the settlers erected new cabins out of the arks which had been used as transports by the army, and the pickets and block-houses of Fort Meigs. This fortress, which had withstood the siege of the British and Indians, was destined to fall before the power of a single individual. The strife to obtain the pickets and irons became cause of serious dissention among the settlers, and to put an end to it, one of them applied a torch to the block-houses and pickets, one dark night, and before daylight, the proud old fort was a heap of smoky ruins.

In 1815, Major Spafford sent to Washington, by his neighbors, to obtain remuneration for the corn which our army had used in the winter of 1813. He succeeded in getting an act passed, which provided for the payment of part of the value of the property destroyed.

One trouble followed another. The lands in the occupancy of the settlers had been purchased, as belonging to the twelve mile reserve, ceded to the United States at the old treaty of Greenville, and were embraced within a parcel of one mile

6

square, which had, by mistake, been ceded a second time, and after the purchase by the settlers, in the treaty of Brownstown. Just after the inhabitants had effected a comfortable settlement, rebuilt their cabins, and planted their crops, an act of Congress was passed, ordering the sale of these lands, leaving the time and place of sale to be fixed by the President. The settlers were now in danger of losing crops, cabins, even the lands themselves, which they had suffered so much to subdue and cultivate. A letter, addressed to President Madison by Major Spafford, under date of March 18th, 1815, describes, in a graphic manner, the losses which he and his neighbors had already sustained, and asks the President to fix the sale of those lands at Fort Meigs, that the settlers may have an opportunity to purchase them. One extract will serve to show how difficult it was to obtain information of public events. It is as follows:

" Should the time not be known, or the place of sale so remote that myself and others could not attend, all would be lost —first, burned by the enemy—secondly, destroyed by our own army, and thirdly, sold by an act of Government to whom we don't know, this would be the last sacrifice, that we could possibly make."

The lands were finally offered for sale at Fort Meigs, and purchased by the settlers without competition. Two considerable towns sprung up at the foot of the rapids, in 1815—one at Fort Meigs, first, called Fort Meigs, and afterwards, Orleans—and the other, at Maumee. This part of the State was then included in Champaign county. Urbana was the County-seat. Fort Meigs was visited by three vessels, in 1815, which came after the Government stores left there at the close of the war. With the exception of a few light vessels, used by the British as transports during the war, these were the first vessels of ordinary draft that ever ascended to the foot of the rapids. The Miami, before spoken of, as the vessel which was captured at Malden, while conveying the ladies of Gen. Hull's army and his papers to Detroit, was built at the foot of the rapids, by Capt. Anderson Martin, in 1810. It was re-captured of the British in the battle of Erie, where it was known by the name of Little Belt. The Chippewa, also captured by the British, was built by Capt. Martin, at Chippewa, in 1810. This was also re-captured at the battle of Erie, and both these vessels, with American troops on board, were afterwards piloted by Capt. Martin to the scene of the decisive victory on the Thames.

In 1816, an Agent was sent by Goverment to locate and survey a town at such point on the river, as seemed most favorable for business purposes. He selected and surveyed the present town of Perrysburg. Among the papers of Major Spafford is the following letter, which doubtless accounts for the name :

WASHINGTON, April 12, 1816.

DEAR FRIEND : As you will have a town on the Miami of Erie, it will be well to think of the name it is to bear. The act does not give a name. Who is to christen it? I wish you would think on the subject and let me know your wishes. For my part, I barely suggest to you that, if it could be called Perrysville or Perrystown, or in some other form which may always remind us of the victory of Erie, it would be good policy. We ought to make the best profit we can of the blood of our countrymen, which has been shed for the confirmation of our independence. If it were left for me to name the town at Lower Sandusky, I should name it in honor of the gallant youth, Croghan, and would say it should be Croghansville. I believe it is in your power to fix the name. Yours, Truly,

JOSIAH MEIGS, }
Comptroller of the Treasury. }

The lots in Perrysburg were exposed to sale at Wooster Land Office in 1817, and many of them purchased by people living in that town, who afterwards settled upon and improved them. The settlement of the town was gradual, at first, but in 1822 the boundaries of Wood county having been determined, it became the County-seat, and rapidly distanced its older neighbors of Maumee and Orleans.

The history of this valley, since it ceased to be the theatre

of warlike achievements, is well enough understood, in its main
features, without a recital. It can be told in the language of
one who, perhaps, had as much to do with it, as any inhabitant.
Major Stickney, in a manuscript biography of himself, says:

"The declaration of war found me in the Indian country, in
the character of an Indian Agent. To the public it would not
appear very well to resign and leave the country. I therefore
continued until the close of the war, rendering such service as
circumstances put in my power to perform. My attention was
soon directed to the country. I began to estimate its capaci-
ty and future prospects. It was a vast, unbroken forest, where
everything was yet to be done, and I was willing to be one to
take hold and aid. I had travelled much in the woods during
the war, and still had to travel in the discharge of my official
duties, but the pressure was diminished, and I had leisure to
review my observations, and saw the importance and practicability of a canal in the vallies of the Wabash and Maumee
rivers. About the time I had arrived at these conclusions, a
number of enterprising and scientific men in Cincinnati, formed
themselves into a society by the name of the Western Emigrant
Society, and created me an honorary member. Their object
was to collect and disseminate knowledge in relation to the
Great West, then but little known. I was invited to furnish
them a communication, containing such observations as I had
made during my residence at Fort Wayne. I wrote some
twenty pages of manuscript, in which, among other details, I
gave my views in relation to the practicability of a canal in the
vallies of the Wabash and Maumee, connecting the two, and
thereby making a water communication from the Gulf of St.
Lawrence to the Gulf of Mexico, with the exception of a portage at the Falls of Niagara."

This communication was published, and a copy of it sent to
Gov. Clinton, who was then maturing his grand project of the
Erie Canal. In a letter which he addressed to Major Stick-
ney in 1818, he writes:—"I have found the way to get into

Lake Erie, and you have shown me how to get out of it."
Again, he writes :—"You have extended my project six hundred miles." In another letter, speaking of the Maumee and
Wabash vallies, he writes :—"That country has now a sparse,
savage population. It must be succeeded by a white, civilized
population, that will be essentially agricultural. On this agri-
culture must rise commerce, and this commerce must have its
concentrating points. Will you have the goodness to give me
a sketch of the country, and, in your judgment, where those
concentrating points will be ? "

Major Stickney, in continuation of his narrative, says :—"In
1817 I was applied to by Gov. Jennings, of Indiana, to assist
in acquiring for the State, the title to the Indian lands. I was
satisfied that no movement towards a canal could take place
without first extinguishing the Indian title to the lands through
which it must pass. I answered the letter by saying, that if
Gov. Jennings would obtain an order from the Secretary of
War, to make the attempt to prepare the Indians of my Agency for a treaty, by which they would relinquish their title to
lands in Indiana, I would cheerfully enter upon the business.
The order soon came from the War Department. I was at this
time corresponding with Gov. Clinton on the subject of a canal from Lake Erie into the valley of the Wabash. In March,
I went to Corydon to visit Gov. Jennings, taking with me my
correspondence with Gov. Clinton. The project of a canal
electrified him. After several days discussion of the subject,
and agreeing, upon the most profound secrecy, we fixed upon
Gov. Cass, Gov. Jennings and Judge Park as Commissioners
for the contemplated treaty. I returned to Fort Wayne to
prepare the Indians, and in April reported to the War Department the probable practicability of the extinguishment of the
Indian title to the lands in Indiana."

" During the negotiation of the treaty at St. Mary's, Gov.
Jennings, Judge Park and myself were very busily engaged in
discussing the merits of the projected canal, the ground to be

occupied, the difficulties to be overcome, and the ways and means generally. What we most feared was, that if the State of Ohio supposed there was any such matter seriously contemplated, they would oppose it. After the close of the treaty, by which, with the exception of a few special reservations, the entire Indian title in Indiana was ceded to the Government, we kept the subject alive by correspondence."

" With me, the canal had now become a settled matter. In view of the practicable results resting upon the execution of the work, I had determined, for myself, the eastern termination near the mouth of the Maumee, and in pursuance thereof, located near the spot where the commercial city of Toledo now stands. This locality, at that time, was considered to be in the Territory of Michigan—the Black Swamp having, from convenience or some similar cause, been designated the northern boundary of Ohio. The people of Ohio had but little communication north of it; but westerly, they claimed that it extended far enough to include Fort Wayne. The whole of the northern and half of the western boundary of Ohio had not then been run. There was about one hundred miles square of the State of Ohio, to which, as late as 1817, the Indian title had not been extinguished."

"In 1795 Gen. Wayne, at the Greenville treaty, made a reservation of twelve miles square, from their country, for military and commercial purposes. The centre of this reserve was the Big Island, at the foot of the rapids of the Maumee. This reservation extends down the river far enough to include the mouth of Swan Creek, and a part of the ground now occupied by the city of Toledo."

" By a special act of Congress, in the session of 1816–17, this reserve was ordered to be surveyed and sold in February 1817. A company of men, residing principally in Cincinnati, purchased, at the auction, two tracts, making about four hundred acres, at the mouth of Swan Creek, laid out a few town lots, and called it Port Lawrence. They offered a part of their lots for sale at auction, in September 1817, at the Indian treaty of Fort Meigs. I was the purchaser of a greater number of lots than any other person. I then conceived that this property was to constitute a part of the future commercial city."

"The company had purchased these lands of the United States upon the conditions of paying one-fourth in hand and the remainder in three equal annual payments, and had sold on the same terms. After the first payment, in consequence of the revulsion of money affairs, they found themselves unable to pay the other instalments, they having agreed to pay for the Port Lawrence tract, seventy-six dollars and six cents per acre. Congress passed a law for their relief, called " The Relief Law," by which they were allowed to relinquish a part to the United States, and to apply the amount of the quarter payment upon the three instalments, for the part they chose to retain. Under this provision, the Port Lawrence tract was entirely relinquished. All the lots that had been sold, were surrendered to the United States. I prosecuted the Company on their contract with me, and obtained a compromise. Before the surrender, I had made brick to build a dwelling on the lots I had purchased. These, I now removed on a large tract adjoining, which I had purchased some years before, and built a house there, and commenced making a farm, determined to live by farming until the canal should be made."

"There was, at this time, a corporate body in the State of Michigan, known by the name of the University of Michigan, which owned some floating sections that the United States had given them for the purpose of a University. They had a right to locate on certain lands within the Territory of Michigan belonging to the United States. The Port Lawrence tract was considered as being within the territory, but not exactly of the description called for. However, they located upon these two tracts, and their title was subsequently confirmed by act of Congress."

"The Cincinnati Company was deemed to be dead. Three

of the gentlemen who belonged to it, still having a high opinion of the Port Lawrence tracts, entered into a negotiation with the University of Michigan, by which they became the owners of this important piece of ground. The gentlemen were Martin Baum, William Oliver (the young officer, whose exploits are recorded in the early part of this history,) and Micajah T. Williams."

"The growth and prosperity of the contemplated city depended so much upon the success of the project for the canal, that I skip over a period of several years, during which, there was nothing of moment occurred in the history of the country, and come down to 1827. All the difficulties in the way of the canal, now appearing to be removed, at the suggestion of Gov. Jennings and myself, a petition was presented in Congress, through Messrs. Hendricks and Test, Representatives from Indiana, praying that the Government would grant to the State of Indiana the alternate five miles square of land on each side of the line of a canal from the navigable waters of the Wabash to Lake Erie. It was laughed at as a wild and visionary scheme, wholly impracticable, and this feeling protected it from opposition, and secured the grant, which was made immediately. Congress had no idea of the importance of their action. The members from Ohio did not think of its touching Ohio or Michigan. The grant was made to the infant State of Indiana, as a play-thing would be given to a child. Soon, the State of Indiana began to make such demonstrations, that the citizens of Ohio, for the first time, discovered that the canal was to pass through a part of their State. They arrayed themselves against the improvement, and declared it an outrage, that Congress should grant power to one State to make a canal, for their accommodation, through another."

"The southern and eastern parts of Ohio, only, were, at this time, inhabited—and the inhabitants of these portions opposed everything that promised to lead to a speedy settlement of the north-west part of the State, from a spirit of rivalry. Opposition from this source had been foreseen by the original movers in the canal project. The Buckeyes said to the Hoosiers, that the United States might give them land to make a canal in Ohio, but they could not give them the government of it. This operated as a check to Indiana."

"There was, at this time, one member of the Ohio Legislature of great political influence, who did not sympathize with the narrow views of his brother members. Many years before, he had consulted with me in relation to the canal. He saw through the whole matter, and acknowledged the importance of the great work to both States. This was Micajah T. Williams. He favored the views of Indiana, which State, it was plain to be seen, could not aggrandize herself at the expense of Ohio. She was also willing to relinquish her right to so much of the lands, included in the grant by Congress, as lay in Ohio, on condition that Ohio would construct that portion of the canal that traversed her territory. In this state of things, Mr. Williams seized the subject with the grasp of a giant, and by excellent management, conciliated the favor of a sufficient number of members of the Legislature to effect, in a single year, a compromise between the two States, the terms of which were, that Indiana should surrender to Ohio the lands granted for canal purposes, in Ohio, and our State, in consideration therefor should construct the canal through them. This arrangement was ratified by special act of Congress, and Ohio, though still reluctant to undertake the work, waited until forced to do it, and then did it well."

" In 1832, seeing no prospect that Baum and Oliver would make any advances in improvement on their grounds at the mouth of Swan Creek, I closed with an offer made to me by Mr. Samuel Allen, of Lockport, New York, by which improvements were to be commenced upon my land. Allen was a shrewd, far-seeing man, and had discovered the importance of the location, some years before this time. A contract was entered into between us, by the terms of which, Allen was to re-

7

ceive half the ground, upon the performance of certain cove-
nants therein set forth. This was in October, 1832, and the
contract run until the following January. Allen failed to perform his part of the contract, but came on, in January, bringing with him a gentleman by the name of Otis Hathaway,
whom he desired might be taken into partnership, and a new
contract made. This was done, and a town plat was laid out,
and called Vistula, but owing to pecuniary difficulties, all action under this contract was suspended in a short time. Allen
bought Hathaway's interest, and a new contract between us
was entered into, by the terms of which, we were to commence
building wharves, warehouses and dwelling-houses in the town,
expend considerable sums in making certain roads leading to
and from it, and perform other acts, in all, involving an ex-
penditure of about $30,000. One-half of this expenditure was
to be made in six months. From some cause, Allen failed to
comply with the contract, and after six months, I offered the
property for sale, and put an end to it. Allen returned to
Lockport, but after a few months, came back, accompanied by
Edward Bissell, Esq., with whom I entered into a contract similar to the one made with Allen."

"Bissell set about the work of improvement in earnest. He
built wharves and houses, advanced money for making roads,
and in many respects, did more than his contract required.
Vistula advanced rapidly and soon acquired considerable repu-
tation."

"In the meantime, Martin Baum died, and William Oliver and
Micajah T. Williams were deemed the surviving proprietors of
the adjoining ground, where a town plat had been laid out in
1817. They took advantage of the improvement in Vistula
and made some improvements in Port Lawrence."

"In 1833, Port Lawrence and Vistula, now united under the
name of Toledo, were, as claimed by Michigan, both within her
boundaries. Ohio had made some faint pretensions to a right
to extend her boundary north, to a line established by Con-

gress. Just as the rival claims of Ohio and Michigan, were ripening into a contest between the two sovereignties, work was commenced upon the Wabash & Erie Canal in Indiana, which was followed by surveys of that work in Ohio. The people began, for the first time, to see the importance of the eastern terminus of this great work, and flocked, in considerable numbers, to the valley. Towns began to rise on the Maumee; some eight plats were laid out upon the estuary of the Maumee, each claiming to be the particular point most to be benefitted by the canal. Ohio began to enquire into her rights, in relation to her northern boundary. Her first movement was to claim taxes to Harris' line. Resistance was made to the claim. The taxes were not paid. I was appointed Justice of the Peace by the Territory of Michigan, to defend the inhabitants against the exactions of Ohio."

" By the ordinance of 1787, it is provided that the territory north-west of the Ohio should be divided into not less than three States, nor more than four; that the eastern State (Ohio) might be extended north so far as to take in a part or the whole of the territory, to the British boundary, if Congress should see fit; but, in case of making only three States, the northern line of the eastern State should be drawn due east, from the southern boundary of Lake Michigan, until it should strike the Miami Bay or Lake Erie."

" When the territory had been permitted to form a constitution in conformity to this line, and become a State, and the Convention had assembled at Chillicothe for the purpose of making the Constitution, there happened to be there a man by the name of Wells, who had been long a prisoner with the Indians residing in this region, who told the members that Lake Michigan would be found to be much farther south than was supposed. This induced the Convention to introduce a provision into their constitution, to the effect that, if a line drawn due east from the southern bend of Lake Michigan should strike the Maumee River or Bay before it should strike Lake Erie, then, and in that case, it should be so run, that a line drawn from the southern extreme of Lake Michigan should strike the North Cape of Maumee Bay."

" Provision was made for surveying the lines between Ohio and Indiana, so far as they had not been run, and between Ohio and Michigan. Leave was necessarily asked of the Indians, as the lines must be run through their territory, which could not be done during the war. Gov. Cass ordered me to obtain the consent of the Indians, and I did so, by assembling them in 1816, for that purpose, and reported the same to the General Land Office. Soon after this, a Mr. Harris was sent out, as Deputy Surveyor, to run the remaining part of the western and the northern lines of Ohio. He was sent to me to learn his starting points and to be furnished with Indian guides, &c. He showed me his instructions, and I reported the tenor of them to Gov. Cass. When Mr. Harris had completed his survey, he went to Detroit, and by request showed Gov. Cass the instructions he had received from Surveyor General Tiffin. Gov. Cass perceived that the Surveyor General had taken the Constitution of Ohio for his guide, in framing his instructions, instead of the ordinance of 1787. He immediately made complaint to the President. President Monroe gave the Surveyor General a rap over the knuckles, and ordered him to send another deputy to run a line due east from the southern extreme of Lake Michigan, according to the views of Gov. Cass. The next year, a Deputy Surveyor by the name of Fulton, was sent to run a line due east. This laid the foundation of what has been called the Toledo war."

" The question as to which of those lines was to be considered the true one to divide the territory, was not much mooted for a number of years. A few letters passed between the Governor of Ohio and the Governor of Michigan upon the subject. Several times it was introduced in Congress, but it was a question they were unwilling to agitate, and no decision was had. At length, Indiana having made considerable progress with the

Wabash & Erie Canal, in her State, called aloud upon Ohio to perform her part of the contract. In 1824, Ohio began to manifest a disposition to move in this enterprise, and likewise to extend her Miami Canal from Dayton to Lake Erie, in communication with the Wabash & Erie Canal. During this year, Micajah T. Williams, one of the Canal Commissioners, with Samuel Forrer, as Engineer, took a level from Cincinnati to the Lake, and examined Maumee Bay."

" Ohio began to see the importance of this disputed piece of land between the two lines, they being about eight miles apart on the shore of Lake Erie. It was evident that where the united canals, which traversed the two richest vallies in the west, terminated, a great commercial city must arise. The idea that Michigan should control this location—this great distributing office of the commerce of the west, was not to be endured. Ohio wanted it, to develop it—Michigan wanted it, to prevent its development. She was aware that if properly improved, it would injure Detroit and ruin Monroe. As Ohio pressed her claims upon Congress, Michigan grew belligerent, and declared a determination to fight, sooner than yield an inch. The few inhabitants on the disputed ground, saw themselves between two fires. I was often applied to for advice, and urged all to stand by Ohio, as the only safety. The Michigan leaders, seeing this, pounced upon me as the head and front of the offending. I found that I was not only chosen defendant, but must submit to the choice. We were all desirous that the question should be speedily settled, that we might know where we were. With very few exceptions, we saw that it was our interest to belong to Ohio."

"In the midst of these disputes, the great question arose, where the Wabash & Erie Canal should terminate. Ohio had control of this matter, and it was not to be doubted, would make the termination in Ohio. If Congress should decide that the southern or Fulton line was the boundary, the mouth of the Maumee, and the spot now occupied by Toledo, would be within the Territory of Michigan, and if the northern, or Harris line was fixed upon, they would be in Ohio. Ohio delayed all action in relation to the canal, until Congress should determine the boundary. It was not the extent of territory, but the spot most convenient for the commercial city, that constituted the importance of the question at issue. I had considered the project of the Wabash & Erie canal the great object of my life, and next to it, in importance, was the point I had made choice of for the termination. Congress was reluctant to take up the question. It required some great excitement to force it upon them, and delay could not be submitted to without serious consequences—the canal would be kept back, and, of course, the town. Interest was at stake—our pockets were touched. We could not but feel great anxiety, on account of both town and canal."

" In the fall of 1833, I determined to attend the ensuing session of Congress, to do what might be in my power to urge on a decision of the important question. The session of the Ohio Legislature, of the Legislative Council of Michigan and of Congress met about the same time. Through the aid of a confidential friend, and for the purpose of getting up what I conceived to be the necessary excitement, I caused a suggestion to be made to several of the members of the Legislative Council, to the effect that they might derive great benefit from the passage of a law, inflicting heavy pains and penalties upon any who should acknowledge any other authority, than such as should be derived from the territory, within her limits. Soon after my arrival at Washington, I was informed that the plan had taken well, and that a bill of a very strong character, was drawn and passed, with one or two dissenting votes. There was in the Legislative Council, Daniel S. Bacon, a man of more coolness and forecast than the rest, who saw the effect that would be likely to follow. He prevailed upon the Council to re-consider or lay on the table. Bacon wrote his views of the matter to Austin E. Wing, who was then at Washington as an

Agent for the territory. Wing consulted Gen. Cass, then Secretary of War. They agreed with Bacon, and Wing, with the assistance of Cass, wrote Bacon a very able letter, denouncing the bill of Pains and Penalties. This was shown to the Council and it put the bill to rest. Bacon wrote Wing another letter, extolling his services very highly for having written so fine a letter. Proud of his performance, and not being aware of my plans and views, Wing read to me the entire correspondence. Lucius Lyon was then delegate in Congress from the territory. He was a man of warm, impetuous temperament and moderate forecast. The Governor and a majority of the Legislative Council of Michigan, were of the same pattern. Lyon had much more influence with them than such men as Wing and Bacon. I requested three members of Congress, friends of mine, to have a conversation with Lyon, and make the impression upon him, that some immediate and decisive action was necessary on the part of Michigan, to determine Congress to decide the boundary question in their favor. Lyon took the bait, and wrote immediately to the Council at Detroit, urging them to pass the bill of Pains and Penalties. It was passed, with no other opposition than that of Bacon.

"The Legislature of Ohio, being now in session, as soon as the mail could carry the proceedings of the Michigan Council to Columbus, it kindled a fire as violent as any of us could have desired. It worked even better than we had anticipated. The Legislature authorized the Governor to call out ten thousand militia ; placed between two and three hundred thousand dollars at his command to defray the expenses ; authorized him to appoint Commissioners to re-mark the Harris line, appoint executive officers, and organize government on the disputed territory, &c. The fire soon reached Washington. A warm correspondence ensued between the Secretary of State and the Governor of Ohio. A young hotspur by the name of Mason was the acting Governor of Michigan. He showed but little disposition to be under the control of the general Government.

"Our Governor, Lucas, appointed Commissioners to re-mark the line, and ordered out five hundred militia to protect them, which he led in person to the Maumee River. While he was here, and the commissioners a few miles off running the line, they were fired upon by a party of militia from Michigan, who took some of them prisoners, and the others made good their retreat. This ended the re-marking for the time."

"At this time, President Jackson sent out Commissioners Rush and Howard, to the disputed territory to endeavor to effect a compromise between Ohio and Michigan. They proposed terms, to which Ohio acceded, but the youngster would not."

"Soon after the organization of government on the disputed territory, under the authority of Ohio, an election was required to be holden, and an assemblage of the people took place at Toledo. A question immediately arose as to who dared to be the officers of said election, in the face of the bill of Pains and Penalties, passed by the Legislative Council of Michigan. The assembled citizens looked for a long time very seriously at each other. At length, at my request, they elected me one of the judges. Any of them were ready, after my election, to fill the other vacancies. Accordingly, Platt Card and John T. Baldwin were elected. This constituted a very full challenge of the authorities of Michigan, and increased the excitement necessary to bring Congress to some decisive action. It was the occasion of a very great noise in Ohio and Michigan, and in fact, I may say, throughout the United States. The citizens of the two neighboring towns, Maumee and Perrysburg, under the impression that if Michigan retained the disputed territory, the canal would terminate at Maumee, took sides with Michigan."

"The ten thousand troops were organized according to the orders of the Governor of Ohio, and held in readiness to march to the frontiers, to protect our boundary, at a moment's notice."

"I attended the session of Congress of 1834–5, to urge on the interests of Ohio, the Wabash & Erie Canal and the town of Toledo, so far as they might be effected by a settlement of the boundary question favorable to our State. The Senate decided in favor of Ohio, by a vote of 30 to 10. In the House, it was referred to a select committee, of which Hon. John Quincy Adams was chairman. No one had any knowledge of which side he was on. When the report was made, it was ascertained that he was determinedly set in favor of Michigan. He had been so silent, that he was agreed upon by both parties. There was but a bare majority on the committee in favor of Michigan. He made a most violent speech. He said the claims of Michigan "were established as strong as the laws of God."

At the close of the session of Congress, in March, 1835, I returned to Toledo. Not long after, I was on a visit of friendship at Monroe. The authorities of Michigan thought it a favorable opportunity to make a display of their vengeance against me for taking the part of Ohio in the great contest, and with great display, they seized me and threw me into prison, on a criminal action founded on the law of Pains and Penalties—of which I have already given the history—and specifically, for acting as Judge of an election at Toledo, under the authority of Ohio. They demanded very heavy bail of me, for my appearance, which I at first refused to give, but after annoying them awhile, I procured bail, and came out."

" A few individuals on the disputed ground adhered to Michigan. They made a Justice of the Peace and some other small officers there, through whom, they contrived to harass the people with petty lawsuits. Even criminal prosecutions were commenced against such as ventured to speak against the claims of Michigan. A son of mine (Two Stickney, Esq.,) dared openly to question the authority of Michigan, and an officer, (Joseph Wood, Esq.,) was sent from Monroe to Toledo to arrest him as a criminal. Young Stickney refused to be taken, and bid the officer defiance, ordering him to preserve a certain distance, or he would pierce him with a dagger. The officer advanced and was stabbed—the first and only blood shed dur-

8

ing the war. At first, the wound was supposed to be mortal, but it did not prove so. Young Stickney retired to the interior of Ohio. Michigan requested the President to order the Governor of Ohio to give him up. Gen. Jackson made the order, but Governor Lucas plainly told him, that the whole military power of the United States should not force him to comply with the order. Young Stickney remained at Columbus, under the protection of Governor Lucas, who gave him assurances of protection, if to do so, required him to call out his ten thousand men."

"It was with great difficulty that Gov. Lucas was prevented, on several occasions during the contest, from taking the field with his large military force. Such a circumstance, owing to the great disparity between the great State of Ohio and the Territory of Michigan, would have arrayed public sympathy against Ohio, and injured her prospects for a favorable decision of the question. Our policy, therefore, and the one which we carried out, was to excite Michigan to the greatest acts of assumption and foolish resistance, and make as few demonstrations as possible on the part of Ohio."

"Governor Mason was a smart young man, of great impetuosity, and he had many men of similar character in authority about him. In July, 1835, he sent a military force of two hundred and fifty men to Toledo to take young Stickney. They ransacked my house, breaking doors, eating, destroying property, menacing myself and family, aiming at me with a loaded rifle, and firing it in the direction where Mrs. Stickney stood. Not finding my son, they concluded to arrest me, and accordingly dragged me off with great violence. Mrs. Stickney accompanied me. We walked about a mile and were then thrust into a lumber wagon and drawn two or three miles. Here, a friend of mine offered me his private carriage. A consultation was held, as to the propriety of permitting me to accept the offer. Finally, the commanding officer* came up and decided the question, and we were permitted not only to ride

---

* Col. Warner Wing.

in the carriage, but I was allowed to drive. Here the superior officers began to show signs of wishing to get rid of their prisoner, but the rank and file thought it a good opportunity to punish the "old rascal." I was perfectly passive. They were conducting the business perfectly to my satisfaction. The procession now began to move. I had two armed out-riders on each side of the carriage to prevent me from escaping. In about two miles, one of my guards crowded my horse into a mud-hole, where he floundered, fell and would not rise. It became necessary, in order to extricate him, that myself and lady should first be removed, and the guards, in order to accomplish this, were under the necessity of wading through mud two or three feet deep, and transporting us upon their backs to dry land. We were now again thrust into a lumber wagon and moved on, leaving a party to get out the horse and carriage. About ten miles from Toledo, at eleven o'clock at night, we halted to remain for the night. Some were for guarding us with great care—others, of more discernment, were for contriving means to return with us to Toledo. It was not long before the horse and carriage came up. The party that wished to get rid of us, being the strongest, proposed to me that my carriage should be brought to the door, and myself and lady should get in, and they would turn the head of the horse towards Toledo. I declined, of course, for this would end the farce."

" The next morning, (Sunday,) at eight o'clock, a coach and four were brought up, and Mrs. Stickney and myself seated in it. A guard of two, with fixed bayonets, were placed in the carriage with us. In this style, we drove into Monroe, and halted in front of the principal hotel, where there were hundreds assembled. The leaders in the great drama were there, his excellency the Governor, and the general* in command under him, were said to be in the house, but did not appear in the crowd. Some of the principal citizens of Monroe came around the carriage, and pressed us to get out of the carriage and go

* Gen. Joseph Brown.

into the house. It appeared evident that they were mortified and disappointed, and wished to make a joke of it. I thought I understood the game better than to treat it as a trifle. I demanded that as I was brought there as a prisoner, I should be treated as such and committed to prison. They declined committing me, urged us to get out, and finally took the horses from the carriage. At length, a mob appeared which threatened to upset the coach. The more respectable, fearing that they might put their threats into execution, consented that I might be committed to prison. Mrs. Stickney insisted upon accompanying me, and we were both locked up in the jail of the county. Breakfast was ordered and served up there. It was not long before an officer was sent to inform Mrs. S. that she could not be permitted to remain in prison. She consented to go to the hotel, if they would send a proper escort to conduct her through the mob. The Governor sent his aid to attend to that duty, and she was removed to the hotel."

"I remained in prison until the next day, and was then brought out for examination, and to be informed of the charges against me. After long consultation, these resolved themselves into a complaint for having, when arrested on a former occasion, resisted an officer and kicked him. After a mock examination I was ordered to give bonds in the sum of two thousand dollars. This order being complied with I was discharged, and returned to Toledo."

"The county of Lucas was laid off in 1835, and the 8th day of September of that year, was fixed upon for organizing the County Court, or Court of Common Pleas, at Toledo. The young Governor of Michigan organized a military force of one thousand men, and marched to Toledo, to prevent the Court from assembling. A part of the troops marched into town the night before the Court was to set. Notwithstanding this, the Court assembled and organized a little after sunrise, and adjourned to a school-house without the knowledge of the troops. Gov. Mason received his dismissal from office while he was committing depredations upon the citizens of Toledo. A man by the name of Horner was his successor. The new appointee was so offensive to the hotspurs of Michigan, that they burnt him in effigy and offered him personal insult. This suited Ohio and confirmed President Jackson in his disposition to side with us."

"I attended the session of Congress of 1835–6, and had the gratification, near the close, to witness the final decision of Congress in favor of Ohio."

With this narrative of Major Stickney, we take leave of so much of the history of our valley and city as may not be more properly included in the statistics of its commerce and trade. The Maumee is now not less dear to the Anglo-American race, that have possessed themselves of its borders, than, fifty years ago, it was to Tish-kwa-gwun and his dusky subjects. The little Indian villages have given place to the growing city, and the midnight howl of the wolf is superceded by the equally pro- longed and startling whistle of the locomotive. The faint trail of the native is traversed by the railroad, and the bay and riv- er, once sailed upon by the light canoe only, now bear upon their bosoms the honest and swelling commerce of an immense empire. Where the council-fire burned, now burns the fire of the domestic hearth; where the war-whoop .rung, now rings the church-going bell; where the chiefs met in deadly conclave, now meet the worshippers of the Christian's God, with spirits animated by the Christian's hope. The forest is rapidly fall- ing before the stroke of the woodsman, and change is written upon everything. In vain we look around for our Indian pre- decessors. They have all gone. "They read their doom in the setting sun." Who among us, when he surveys the growth of this valley, in all those elements which constitute true great- ness—who among us, pleasant as it is to linger over the past, would wish to recast the history, or change the destiny which the future is unfolding for this favored region? And yet, in the past, there is a spell-like enchantment, which makes the world around us doubly dear. We love to think that we dwell upon ground once consecrated to the God of battles, in the cause of justice and right. We love to remember that it was here some of those conflicts were fought, which finally achieved that freedom of mind and conscience that constitute our chief heritage. These recollections make our homes dear to us. We recount them with pride, and feel a jealous interest in their preservation from decay. Thus the past is blended with the present, and thus the present swells into the future—that glorious future, rich in its promises of fruition, to the long posterity, that even now, are beginning to enjoy it.